CHAN

WINGS OF HOPE

Library of Congress Control Number: 2017910424
Miller, Jessie.

Chance: Wings of Hope
by Jessie Miller.

Summary: After a strange meeting, a dog and a butterfly discover they have more in common than uncommon.

ISBN 978-0-9991800-0-6 (paperback)

Text and illustrations copyright © 2012 by Jessie Miller.
Published in 2017 by My EPIC Writing, Jacksonville, FL.

For more information about writing and printing please contact:
My EPIC Writing
jessie@myepicwriting.com

Proceeds from the sale of this book go to support the work being done by EPIC Outreach
For More Information about EPIC Outreach please contact:
compassion@epicanimals.org and visit www.epicoutreach.org

INTRODUCTION

 He was called the stray from Miami, Florida, ID #A1436774. Without a name, the gray-and-white pit bull was scheduled to be euthanized.

Do you know what that means? To euthanize is also called "to put to sleep," or the humane killing of an animal. This is often done when there are not enough homes for the number of unwanted animals, or if an animal is suffering medically or has a behavioral issue that is unsafe or cannot be changed.

Thanks to social media and grassroots efforts to save lives, Chance—as he soon was renamed—went from being abandoned, hungry, and lost, to quickly settling into the home that rescued him.

In his high-spirited curiosity, he stumbled upon an interesting creature, which proved to teach a valuable lesson. Together they shared each other's struggle.

Be Kind
To yourself because kindness creates love and you are a loveable being.

"Who are you?" Chance asked, bouncing up and down, trying to get a closer look at the odd flying creature.

Zigzagging back and forth from one colorful flower to another, the busy flying thing had no time to be bothered by a pesky dog.

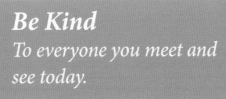

Be Kind
To everyone you meet and see today.

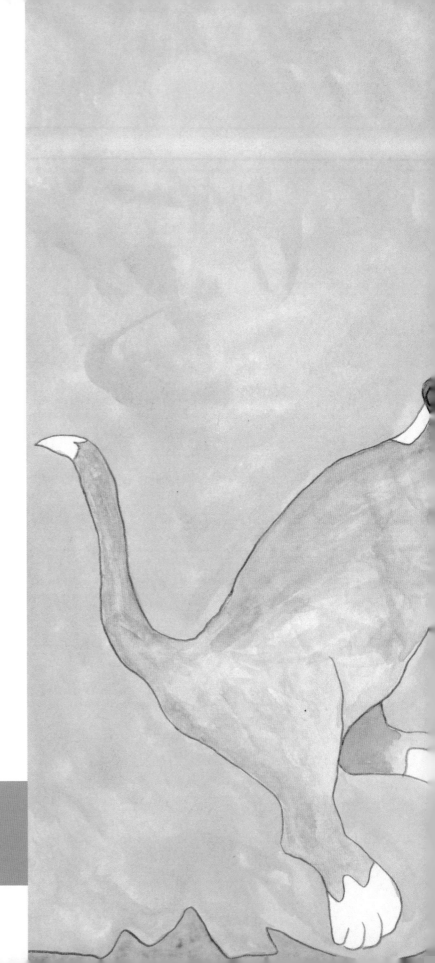

Chance barked louder, saying, "Where are you going?"

Continuing to flutter his wings this way and that way, across and over, around and around, the critter flew about the overgrown plant.

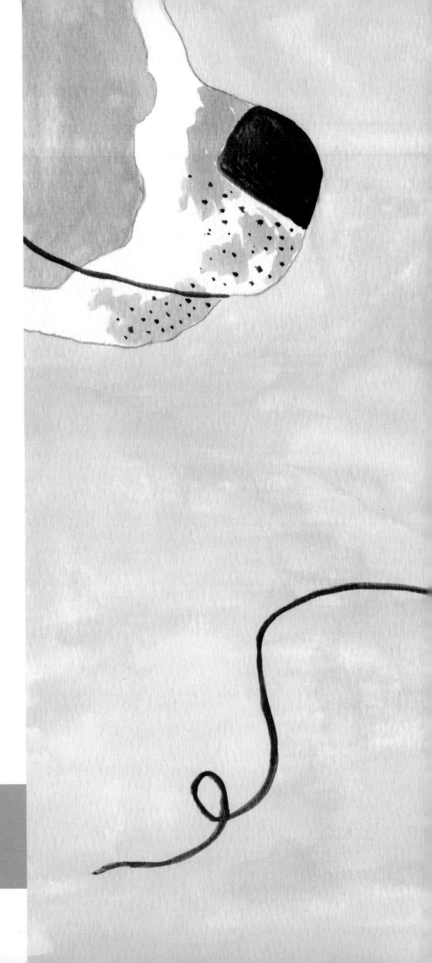

Be Kind
No matter what others are doing.

Persistent and pestering, Chance wasn't giving up on his quest to learn about the silly winged creature.

"What are you?" Chance growled, boldly barking and demanding an answer. "And what is your name?"

"I am a butterfly," said the gold, orange, and black creature. "A monarch butterfly, to be specific." He sounded grouchy when he added, "And my name is Fletcher."

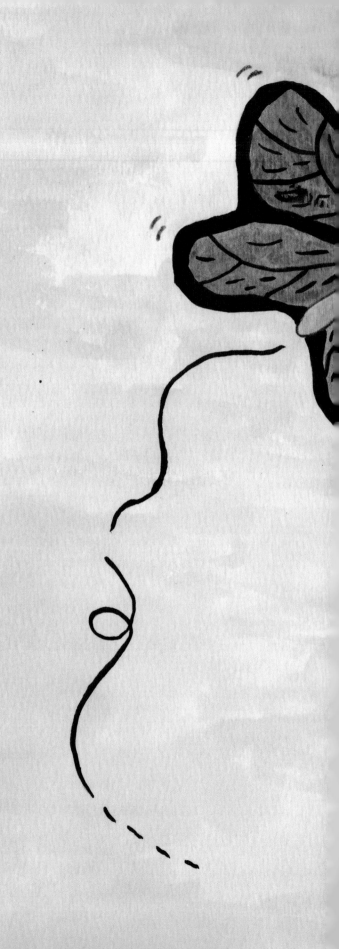

Chance barked, "Stop moving so fast!"

Fletcher flapped his shiny wings, making a sharp turn and soaring straight toward Chance's wondering face.

"What is it with your curiosity, kid?" Fletcher grumbled, and then he landed on the tip of Chance's wet nose.

Be Kind
Even if you don't want to.

10

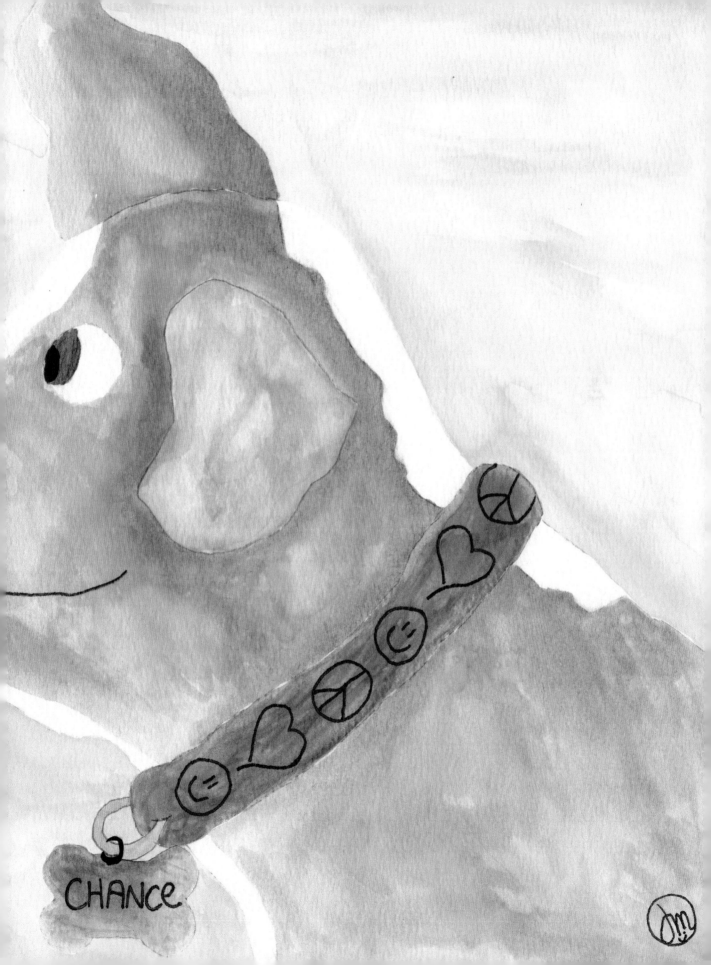

Chance replied, "I have never seen a bug like you before."

"Don't call me a bug. I am an interesting and intelligent insect," Fletcher stated. "As I said, a butterfly. Besides, what kind of dog are you, all gray and white? You look like a marble."

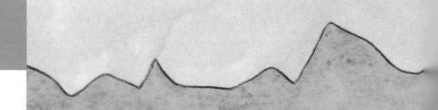

Chance sat for a moment, staring at Fletcher. The butterfly reminded him of a stained-glass window Chance had once seen.

"Well, I am an all-American dog," he barked. "A happy, friendly, people-pleasing American Staffordshire Terrier."

Fletcher fell backward, onto the ground, in uncontrollable laughter. "Ha-ha! … You're a pretty funny dog."

After catching his breath from the bellyaching chuckle, the butterfly snickered, "I think you mean you're a pit bull."

Be Kind
As if there isn't any other option.

Chance lowered his head, and his eyes drooped. "Yes, I am a *pit bull*, but I am not a bad dog."

"Of course you're not. Who said you're a bad dog?" Fletcher asked.

"Most people," Chance replied. "When they hear the words *pit bull*, they run away, thinking I am going to hurt them."

Chance lay down and Fletcher crawled onto one of his furry paws.

Chance said, "I guess they are afraid of my breed. Can you believe anyone is afraid of me?"

Be Kind
Think good thoughts, say nice things, and do good deeds.

Fletcher giggled, and said, "You? Hurt anyone? That is silly. You're so goofy and clumsy, you couldn't hurt me if you tried."

Be Kind
Because it's the right thing to do.

Fletcher spread his large wings and wrapped them around Chance. "Don't worry, kid. Most people think I am a bug even though I am an insect."

Fletcher sighed. "If only people would get to know us," he said.

"You mean without judging us by our appearance?" replied Chance.

"That's right," Fletcher said.

Be Kind
And those around you will be kinder too.

24

"I know," Chance replied, quickly jumping to his feet and standing tall and proud. "I might be a pit bull, but I am friendly and playful." He gave a little bark. "And I love to chew on sticks. And spin in circles. I can even sit up for a yummy treat," he declared.

Be Kind
Your heart and brain will thank you.

Fletcher flapped his wings and circled Chance's head. "C'mon, kid. Let's spread our wings and paws," he said.

Chance leaped in the air.

Be Kind
Right now, because you can.

Fletcher flew up and quickly turned and landed on Chance's nose again.

With his wings spread wide, Fletcher yelled, "You live and act as a happy and friendly pit bull, and I will fly with grace and glory as a beautiful butterfly."

Fletcher flew off into the bright sunshine and Chance leaped after him, ears bouncing and tail wagging.

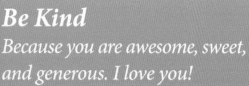

Be Kind
Because you are awesome, sweet, and generous. I love you!

Critical Thinking Questions for Students

1. What does it mean to judge someone or something?

2. What is discrimination?

3. Do you think Chance and Fletcher feel discriminated against?

4. How do you think it feels to be judged or discriminated against?

5. Have you ever felt discriminated against or judged for something?

6. What are some ways we can make people and animals feel not discriminated against?

7. How can you make someone or something feel welcome or liked?

Be Kind
Be caring, be loving, be tolerant.

Tips and Talking Points for Teachers, Parents, and Guardians

Breed-specific legislation (BSL) is discrimination against a specific breed of dog. As of 2017, Miami, Florida, has a BSL in place for pit bulls. This means that any dog resembling or labeled as a pit bull cannot be adopted out from the city shelter and they are euthanized ("put to sleep").

Pit bulls are not the only breed facing this challenge. It is a serious matter affecting millions of dogs across the globe, in communities and animal shelters every day.

Like humans, who should not be judged by race, religion, or sexual orientation, dogs should not be judged by their breed. Each dog is an individual with a unique background and personality—just like people. Humans are classified by race, such as Caucasian, African American, or Chinese. Dogs are grouped by breed, such as pit bull, German shepherd, poodle, or Chihuahua. Remove the breeds and races and you are left with individual dogs and human beings.

Each one of us has a gift and a purpose to offer the world. When we recognize those gifts, we honor the beauty in each living thing. Together, we can begin a major change by seeing the gifts each human being and animal has to offer the universe.

When we stop discriminating based on outside appearances, our world becomes harmonious, peaceful, joyful, and loving. Living a life open and accepting—with no limitations on people, places, or things—encourages compassion, kindness, peace, and, ultimately, love.

Join me in creating a compassionate world by **being kind** to everyone and everything!

Be Kind
You and all things deserve it.

About Chance

Chance is a real dog rescued off the streets of Miami, Florida, in 2012. He was lucky to get a "freedom ride" out of the high-kill shelter that he was brought into after being found as a stray. His original name was Tank, and after fostering him for about a month, he was quickly renamed Chance because he got a second chance at life! When he first came into foster he was skinny, sick, and had to be nurtured and loved before he started feeling better. Today, Chance is happy and healthy and lives a life of luxury with several playmates including dogs, cats, and often a pocket pet like a rat or a guinea pig (depending on what Mom has rescued). In the photos is Chance's adopted brother, Wrigley.

About EPIC Outreach

EPIC Outreach is a nonprofit 501(c)(3) that exists to inspire compassion by sharing information through humane education, networking, and outreach, to create a kinder world for people, animals, and the environment. EPIC Outreach was founded and created in 2015 and is not a rescue, but an education outreach organization that focuses on sharing information to inspire change and have an impact that lasts. EPIC Outreach reaches children (our future) and teaches through engaging curriculum, games, and art projects about being kind to animals, each other, and the environment. Also, EPIC helps people and pets in underserved communities by providing food and

resources directly to the people and animals. Since being founded, EPIC Outreach has spoken to more than 1,500 children on being kind to animals, people, and the environment, along with providing food to pets, helping to network and save the lives of several long-term shelter pets.

About the Author

Jessie Miller is an avid animal advocate who loves to write and educate. She is an animal enthusiast and runs a nonprofit, EPIC Outreach, which focuses on rescue, service, and humane education outreach. EPIC teaches compassion for people, animals, and the environment. Jessie has more than twenty years' experience handling pets (cats, dogs, and small animals such as rabbits, rats, guinea pigs, and more). She also has hands-on experience in rescue and education with wildlife, to include snakes, birds, raccoons, opossum, turtles (sea and land), and alligators. As a Humane Society of the United States district leader and a Feral Friend Network partner for Alley Cat Allies, Jessie is on the cutting edge of progressive change for the betterment of people and animals in our communities.

Jessie lives in Florida, where she spends her time at the beach, running, writing, reading, and hanging out with her rescued pets: four dogs, five cats, and a rat. Please visit www.epicoutreach.org. You can also read more about her writing at www.myepicwriting.com.

Made in the USA
Columbia, SC
05 April 2018